PLUTO GETS THE CALL

ADAM REX

...and PLUTO was his name-o...

Illustrations

and a bunch of sideline planetary commentary

by Laurie Keller

All right, then. Call him.

NO WAY! I'm not calling him.

Well, don't look at ME!

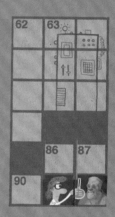

BEACH LANE BOOKS
New York London Toronto Sydney New Delhi

Hi.
NEPTUNE
Hi!
URANUS
VENUS
MARS
THE SUN
Over here! Behind the ice and all those other guys. It's me, Pluto! The ninth planet!

So, not to brag, but I'm mostly made of nitrogen.

Oooh, nitrogen! SWOON!

I'm almost as big as Earth's moon,

PLUTO DIAMETER 1,500 MILES

MOON DIAMETER 2,200 MILES

I'm really cold,

TEMPERATURE -369°F -223°C

CLOSE-UP OF LABEL

HANDMADE BY URANUS

and I have a big heart on my belly 'cause I love being a planet!

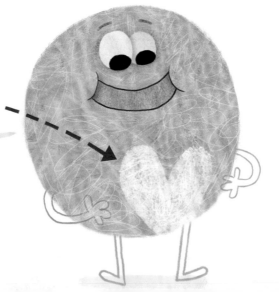

Hold on a second, that's my phone.

You got Pluto!

Oh, what a coincidence—
I was just talking to
someone from Earth!

Sorry,
I should
take this.

Uh-huh.

Uh-huh.

WHAT?

What do you MEAN I'm not a PLANET anymore?

Why am I not a planet anymore?

I...oh... okay, thank you for calling.

That was just some scientists from Earth. They say I'm not a planet anymore, no biggie.

They asked if I'd like to be known as the solar system's largest ice dwarf, and I was like, How'd you like to be known as Earth's... meanest... jerks, huh?

Huh?!

I didn't really say that.

I'm sorry, you were probably hoping to hang out with a *real* planet. Let me show you around.

This is Neptune. He's closer to the Sun than me, but he's still so far away that it takes him 165 years to orbit all the way around! It only takes Earth one year! One year exactly! That's what a year is, actually.

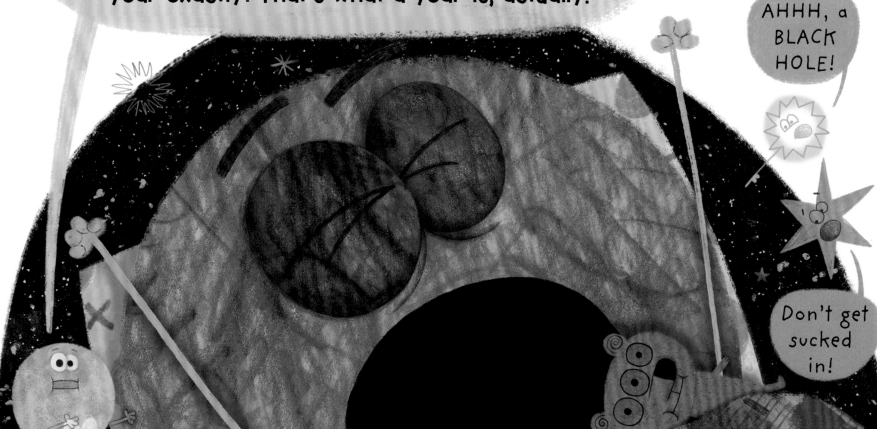

Uranus is icy, too. In fact she and Neptune are called ice giants, which is...

...which is why they want to call me an ice dwarf, I guess.

What's up, Pluto? I know you have kind of a funky orbit, but I don't usually see you this close to the Sun.

These Earth scientists say I'm not a planet anymore.

WHAT?

Hold on, there's my phone—

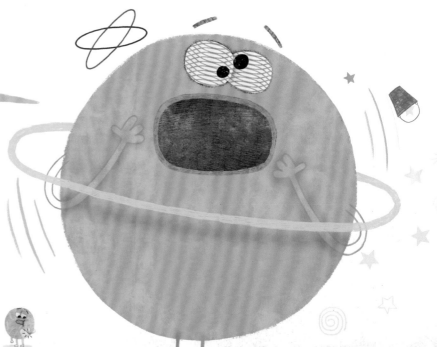

Next up are Saturn and Jupiter. They're gas giants. Again, I am not making these names up.

They look like solid bands from far away, but really they're made up of little bits of ICE and ROCK and DUST.

Oh, stop, stop, stop, **STOP!**

Uh ... hey, look over there! It's Jupiter!

STOP LOOKING AT ME!

Hi, Mars.

I have robots on me.

Yeah?

Some of them just sit there. Some of them roll around.

ROBOTS!

The humans sent them here.

Ugh.

No offense, but I don't want to talk about humans right now.

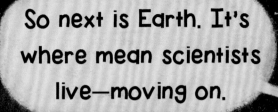

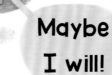

Mercury is the smallest.

And, dare I say, the cutest?

Venus is the hottest.

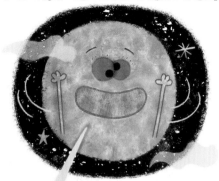

And I rotate in the opposite direction as most everyone else!

Earth has life.

And this yummy sandwich!

Mars has robots.

I guess they're *kind* of cool.

Jupiter's the biggest.

Stop staring at my red spot!

Saturn has its rings.

YOO-HOO! HI, PLUTO!

People talk about Uranus for reasons I don't really want to get into.

Aww, shucks, you must mean my charming personality.

And...well, Neptune is Neptune.

What's THAT supposed to mean?

(close-up of
Pluto's heart)

Meet my fellow dwarf planets: Ceres, Eris, Makemake, and Haumea.

Our solar system formed almost 4.6 BILLION years ago!

PLUTO

AVERAGE DISTANCE FROM THE SUN IN MILES

Mercury – 36,000,000

Venus – 67,000,000

Earth – 93,000,000

Mars – 142,000,000

Jupiter – 484,000,000

Saturn – 886,000,000

Uranus – 1,780,000,000

Neptune – 2,800,000,000

Pluto – 3,670,000,000

SATURN

You're my favorite dwarf planet, Pluto!

MARS

FACT: Saturn has a crush on Pluto!

NUMBER OF DAYS TO ORBIT THE SUN

Mercury – 88

Venus – 225

Earth – 365

Mars – 687

Jupiter – 4,333

Saturn – 10,759

Uranus – 30,687

Neptune – 60,190

Pluto – 90,530

NEPTUNE

I orbited the Sun in 49,000 days once, but boy, did my back pay for it!!

MERCURY

I have no moons or rings, but I have a winning smile, don't you think?

NUMBER OF MOONS

Mercury – 0

Venus – 0

Earth – 1

Mars – 2

Jupiter – 79

Saturn – 62

Uranus – 27

Neptune – 14

Pluto – 5

Oooh, if I can get three more moons, I'll win a free T-shirt!

URANUS

FUN FACTS

WHAT THE PLANETS WERE NAMED AFTER

Mercury – Roman god of travel
Venus – Roman goddess of love
Earth – English/German word for "ground"
Mars – Roman god of war
Jupiter – king of the Roman gods
Saturn – Roman god of agriculture
Uranus – ancient Greek king of the gods
Neptune – Roman god of the sea
Pluto – Roman god of the underworld

APPROXIMATE DIAMETER IN MILES

Mercury – 3,000
Venus – 7,500
Earth – 7,900
Mars – 4,200
Jupiter – 86,900
Saturn – 72,400
Uranus – 31,500
Neptune – 30,600
Pluto – 1,400

They're facts for now, but Science changes all the time!

WHOA! Did Jupiter just get a new moon?

Sol is the Latin word for "sun." That's how our solar system got its name.

The other planets were named after Greek and Roman gods, but I was named after the GROUND?

I have more mass in my little finger than Earth has in her whole body!

A NOTE FROM THE AUTHOR

When I was a kid, there were nine planets—and every list of them ended with Pluto, the little planet farthest from the Sun.

Pluto was discovered by an amateur astronomer named Clyde Tombaugh in 1930. It was named by eleven-year-old Venetia Burney, whose librarian grandfather knew how to get her suggestion to Clyde. At the time, most everyone agreed it was a planet.

But *planet* is just a word, and like any word it only means what we all agree it means. And if we all agree it means "a round object that orbits the Sun," then there's a problem.

Because astronomers have recently discovered other objects that orbit the Sun and are just as round as Pluto. Should they be called planets too? Would twelve planets be okay? What if I told you that astronomers are learning more about our solar system every day, and there might be as many as two hundred of these objects?

Some people might like two hundred planets. Maybe you're one of those people.

But in 2006 astronomers decided on a new definition of the word *planet*: It must orbit the Sun, it must be round, and it should "clear the neighborhood around its orbit." That last bit just means that the planet's gravity ought to either pull smaller objects closer in or throw them out of its way.

Pluto is round and orbits the Sun, but it has a crowded orbit. So it isn't a planet anymore. Today the planets are Mercury, Venus, Earth, Mars, Jupiter, Saturn, Uranus, and Neptune.

People used to say there were twenty-three planets! Then they decided there were nine; now there are eight. Science is always learning, just like you. And sometimes it's stubborn. But Science will always change its mind when it's time—that's what makes it strong. And it's waiting for kids like you to teach it something new.

Whatever I'm called, I'll always be PLUTO!

For Marie, my North Star—A. R.

For Cheese and Olive Moon—
two lucky Space Cats who landed safely in AJ's
living room during the making of this book—L. K.

BEACH LANE BOOKS • An imprint of Simon & Schuster Children's Publishing Division • 1230 Avenue of the Americas, New York, New York 10020 • Text copyright © 2019 by Adam Rex • Illustrations copyright © 2019 by Laurie Keller • All rights reserved, including the right of reproduction in whole or in part in any form. • BEACH LANE BOOKS is a trademark of Simon & Schuster, Inc. • For information about special discounts for bulk purchases, please contact Simon & Schuster Special Sales at 1-866-506-1949 or business @simonandschuster.com. • The Simon & Schuster Speakers Bureau can bring authors to your live event. For more information or to book an event, contact the Simon & Schuster Speakers Bureau at 1-866-248-3049 or visit our website at www.simonspeakers .com. • Book design by Laurie Keller and Lauren Rille • The text for this book was set in KB Pay The Lady. • The illustrations for this book were rendered in traditional, digital, and galactic media. • The Solar System Fun Facts numbers were gathered at https://solarsystem.nasa.gov/. • Manufactured in China • 0819 SCP • First Edition • 10 9 8 7 6 5 4 3 2 1 • Library of Congress Cataloging-in-Publication Data • Names: Rex, Adam, author. | Keller, Laurie, illustrator. • Title: Pluto gets the call / Adam Rex ; illustrated by Laurie Keller. • Description: First edition. | New York : Beach Lane Books, [2019] | Summary: Just after learning that Earth's scientists no longer consider him a planet, an unhappy Pluto takes a visitor from Earth on a tour of the solar system, sharing facts along the way. • Identifiers: LCCN 2018053264 | ISBN 9781534414532 (hardcover : alk. paper).| ISBN 9781534414549 (ebook) • Subjects: | CYAC: Pluto (Dwarf planet)—Fiction. | Planets—Fiction. | Solar system—Fiction. • Classification: LCC PZ7.R32865 Plu 2019 | DDC [E]—dc23 LC record available at https://lccn.loc.gov/2018053264